meet me in the flames

selected horror poetry

by

greg jones

ISBN: 978-1958531853

To my parents who gave me the freedom to dream.

To my daughters, Christina, AnnaMarie and Sophia. This, as with everything, I do for you. I hope I've made you proud.

To my wife, Angela, who has been at my back encouraging me for many years. I know that while my right hand is busy, my left is being held by you.

And to Clive who, when I was 14, kicked open the doors and said "look at what can be done." I never turned away and I haven't looked back.

My love to you all.

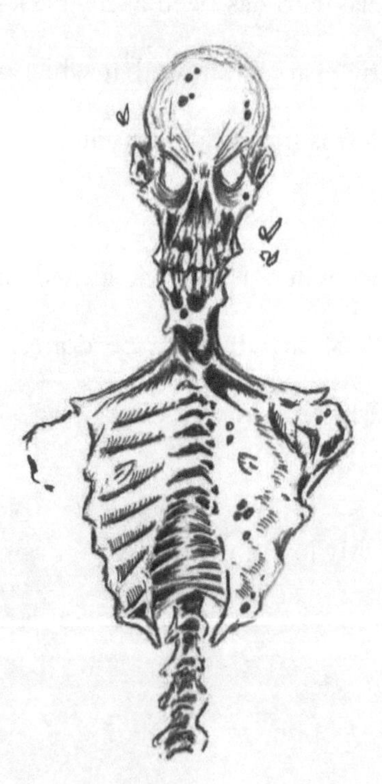

the breath in the body bag

The zipper is thick and catches as I pull it down
The plastic dense and unforgiving
loud in the bright, sterile silence
Down past your pale eyes
teeth separating further
past your slender, shrunken neck
bringing light to the puckered scar running down your
chest, raw and beautiful
I see you once more
brush my fingers along your hollow cheeks
tracing the new severity of your features
I lean in and softly kiss your withered lips
They are damp
and I smile
The zipper is thick and catches as I pull it up

More difficult from the inside

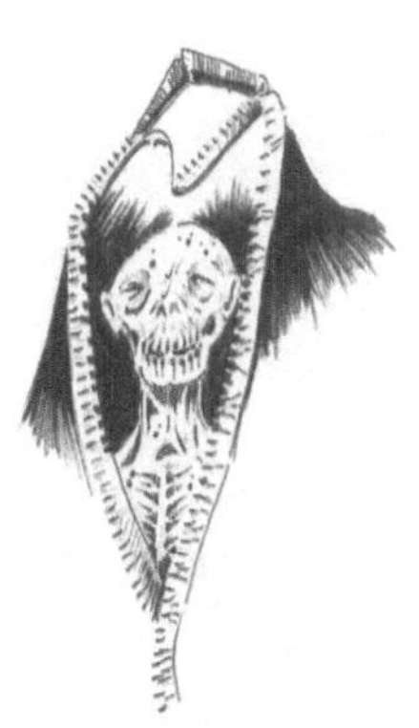

twilight kisses

His mouth is sour
Meat gone bad,
left to spoil on butchers' hooks
Putrid and gray

Lips
pale and cold
thin and waxen

Tongue colder
It swirls in your mouth
A slug left to wilt in the sun
Dry
Grating

Saliva what there is of it,
cold
An afterthought of moisture

You'll find no warmth here

His cheeks do not flush
Pupils do not dilate
No racing of a heart
No panting of breath
It is a one-sided seduction meant for you
A tenderizing of meat for him

You may question the flies
Do not

He watches your pulse
Listens for the space between beats
when the blood is pushed back out from your heart
He lives in that pause

His eyes roll back
Not from pleasure
He is beyond that
His eyes roll and the membrane ascends
Protecting
So as he feeds they are safe from flailing arms and scratch-
ing nails
his teeth make purchase
Your throat opens
Your life drains
and he drinks

For you are food

Nothing more

No chest heaving eternal love
No gothic romance of timeless passion
No taloned midnight caresses or insatiable unquenching
desire

Just food

This then, girls, is the vampire's kiss.
They are dead after all.

the haunted and the harrowed

I see her across the room
Breathing
Warming the night
I approach
Silent
I watch her
Behind the shroud
Grainy white shadows
Subtle grays
I reach for her
Hair lifts from across her eyes
Gossamer strands
Dancing on a cold breath of air
She twitches in her sleep
Her eyes open
Momentarily
she looks into the dark
I think she sees me
She closes her eyes again
Rolls over

The ether takes me
I dissolve into shadow
I'll try again tomorrow

She haunts me

The razors are rusty
a bit dull
overused
They slide into place
Into the end of each finger
the pus helps
They each sit a bit loose at this point
Seems I need the wire more these days
Pain getting worse
but I manage
I have to
I sit up
look in the mirror
smile through the blood
Dirty light hits the new blades
between my teeth
Wire again
Thinner here
but strong

These need to be sharp
for obvious reasons

Weary of being a victim
Of her heart racing
Always cautious
Always in terror
Tired of movement
Watching her children swallowed whole
Tired of being prey
She leads them astray
The hunter
The child
The foolish, feeble fox
So,
with her silken pelt,
her endless eyes,
they follow her innocence
into the deep wood
where the moss grows dark and lush
and another lies waiting
wringing her hands

corners

Look what you did
Wait out in the hall
Stand in the corner
Stare at the wall

So I stood in the corner
with my face to the wall
alone and forgotten
away from them all

The same empty corner
she uses each time
someone acts up
or steps out of line

Did their embarrassment rage
So bright and so red?
at the faces they made?
the words that were said?

I wonder what thoughts
are thought in this place
with tears in your eyes
a blush to the face

Are they the same thoughts
I'm thinking right now?
About getting even
about when, about how?

Did little fingers ache?
Ball into fists?
Longing for throats
to throttle and twist?

Did they hear in their heads
a comforting flick?
Did they envision a room
all sticky and slick?

Then I start feeling better
a little straighter I stand
I stare down with a grin
at the knife in my hand

a satisfied mind

He's always liked the old songs
the simple choruses
the thoughtful lyrics
the plain album jackets with a single photo
Cowboy
Barroom
Pretty girl
Good times
No lyric sheets
You can understand every word
simple
nothing complicated
Innocent
That's the word
It was an innocent time
He smiles
looks at the album
Simple
Just a man in a hat and a sparkly suit
smiling
like him
but… not
More of a grin
Like he knows something
his eyes

Guilty looking in some way
a leer
He's leering
and something niggles in back somewhere
Guilt maybe?
No
He looks again
then over his shoulder
To the bedroom door
album again
then the door
He feels it again
just a faint tug of the conscience
feels the blood coming back into his hand
the ghost of the leather belt fading
He opens and closes his fist
goes to the door
hesitates
So many secrets
So much hidden
Rage
Fear
Disillusionment
It's there
but he doesn't acknowledge it
or the sounds coming from the other side
just grabs the knob
and softly closes the door
He pours a drink
puts the needle down
He sits
reclines
content in his illusion
with a satisfied mind

is someone getting the
best of you?

____

He's reaching for me
Fingers curling
Looking for comfort
We are as one
Tethered
I'm stronger though
I take what is rightfully mine
It was all me at one point
Not long ago
Until the split
When I felt myself siphoned off
Filling what once was void with my essence
Diluting
Dispersing
Eroding
Until I grew hungry
Until Her voice started to fade
My temperature cooling
Until I said enough and began to reclaim myself
I bore down and began siphoning off of him
Pulling nutrients and oxygen and self back into me
I felt his feeble movements
Restricted in this space
Sensed some undeveloped panic coming through the fluid
in tiny ripples
Instinctual
Evolutionary
Until his hand stop reaching

I am not comfort

The ripples fade
All is silent again but the loud thrum of Her heart and the
soft echo of my own
I let it lull me to sleep and pray I don't dream
I grow warm

Forgive me brother

a wall of deeper red

A red painting there hangs
On the wall just ahead
Both the canvas and the frame
Like a wound freshly bled

The wall behind the artwork
A red of deeper hue
The gallery lies vacant
Except for me and you

The colors appear to move
To swirl and to churn
As though eager to reveal
Just what you're here to learn

The closer that you peer
Much deeper run the tones
But to view it I'm afraid
You must approach alone

See there are no brushstrokes
No clear, discernible lines
No artist then can claim it
The work has not been signed

Look deep through the ocher
Your mind you must keep clear
You need a deeper vision
For the image to appear

It's the view of your death, love
No exact time or certain place
Just one fatal, final vision
Of the look upon your face

Is it calm and just serene?
At peace, home in your bed
Or are you screaming out in horror?
At what lies just ahead

Some surprised at the reveal
Not as bad as they had thought
Others clutch hands to their chests,
drop dead right on the spot

Will you look now to this piece
if given half the chance?
Or just quickly leave the room
without a backward glance?

Its draw can be alluring
Its pull won't be denied
That last forbidden knowledge
To learn just how you died

You take a cautious step
Then another and one more
Turning back to look at me
As you slowly cross the floor

   meet me in the flames

I watch you from afar
Gain a look of sheer surprise
You lean in closer just to see
my reflection in your eyes

You turn around to flee
But I block the only door
Then the final veil falls
And you look surprised no more

I glide across the tiles
A slow and easy gait
Knife familiar in my hand,
warm and eager to create

I smile at the painting
Hung a bit askew
It will gain a fresh new shade
Before the night is through

the black bells

From the spire hear the black bells sound
On their ropes, no hand is found
Who do they summon from deep underground?
What comes shambling from the burial mound?
The damned crawl forth for one to be crowned
Hail the Last King, the cheers will resound
To his dark hand your soul to be bound
As still the black bells sound

the thirsty dead

A black tongue rolls over his broken teeth
an un-breath escapes
just dust
and earth
the rotting scraps of our loved ones
He moans
red drips from his slack lips
Those lips
Cold mud peppers my cheek
He looks in my eyes
The light is gone
Just empty
all is blank
but thirst
but hunger
but me
laying beneath him
I pull him down to me
Those broken teeth encircle my mouth
That black tongue finds my own
If my love is to die
let it be by his hand
under his gaze
within our bed

Let him feast

veni in me, inhabitare me

Veni in me
Inhabitare me
Your words carved across my back
my chest
above my heart
stretching skin
forming script
blasphemous
Nintius
whisper to me
things I long to hear
deep inside
I can't see you
but you're there
smiling in the dark
Gratus
Crooked cross on the wall
I welcome
Ama Me
I hold myself
trace your wounds with my fingertips
taste your smoke on my tongue
Frigidus i uri
black light
your laughter echoes
up from caverns

Animus meus
my offering
part my veil of flies
kiss me through the bile
Accipe me
your possession

fear

What's that watching through the trees?
I wonder then just what it sees?

With eye of red and tooth of white
Hungrily staring through the night

Does it sense me watching it?
While my meat roasts on the spit?

So who fears whom as light grows dim?
Him of me or me of him?

crematorium

The dust is on my glasses, in my hair, on my teeth.
I'm breathing it into me nightly.

I imagine it filling me slowly like an hourglass that never tips.
It dances dreamlike across the fluorescent haze.

Settles softly on my eyelashes, the fine hairs on my arms
I rake the grating to reposition the bones and occasionally pull out a
blackened heart
hold it to my ear and listen to its secrets
if it has any stories to tell

I sometimes have to fight the urge to clean my glasses
Blow my nose
but then I think…

These were people
These were dreams and hopes and memories

First kisses and graduations
Heartbreaks and elations
In this ash are lives lived

The bodies that have carried the total experience of a single being
from the piercing of the egg to the final breath of the lungs
The complete absolute journey of a self.

It's humbling
It's glorious.

So I breathe in deep, stifle my cough and light the fires again.

like mothers do

She pulls what remains of her across the splintered floor
Her legs useless
Her pelvis destroyed
She's searching
She drags herself further
hears crying
She pulls her murderer to her arms
Traces blood around her nipple
Winces
as needle teeth attach,
as it feeds
She looks down
into black eyes
and sings
softly
with love
like mothers do

the revolting

I wake to pain
In its entirety
total
Everywhere
        It's dark
am I still sleeping?
      No
My eyelids refuse to open
        Try to pry them apart but my fingers will not move
Neither will my arms
legs
paralyzed
              My eyes!!
My eyes are   pushing
Nudging   out between my lids
Forcing them open
    Some fluid leaks
Their stalks trail down my cheeks
      Warm
I see…
My ears
My lips
The curve of my jaw
      My eyes
they see each other!
They come to rest in the   hollow of my throat
My eyes!

Still observing
        My head!!
Splitting!!
The pain is white
Blinding   white
Searing
Flashbulbs
My skull!
It's   opening
Closing
        Like a fist
Its plates are   separating
Opening
Light finds my mind
The blood comes with the splitt ing of skin
Pouring
Down
Brain fibers   uncoil
Push out my ears
My nostrils
My bladder voids
  Bowels are next
I   gag
Gargle a scream
And choke on my teeth
Tongue is   thrashing in my mouth
Releasing itself
        I feel the roots wetly snap
Then it's gone
My body   spasms
My back   arches and buckles
Then arches again
        My skin burning!
It is coming loose

  meet me in the flames

Stripping
Like curls   of shaved wood
Rolling in ribbons   down my legs
       Pulling away like shreds of green sapling
I'm flaying myself!
J esus!
the pain
Beyond   pain
A new realm
My eyes roll
I see my flesh strips   inch away
       Thick, red worms of self
My muscles disengage
Veins and arteries escape
Un   raveling
         They rise and test the air for the first time
Then follow the route of the flesh
Bones un couple from joints
Lie still in the wet dark
Each now an individual   entity
    Free from the collective
Blood   comes
And   goes
Pooling
Spread   ing
Out and   away
In rivulets
Then rivers
I'm cold   now
I pass out somewhere
         Somewhen
Wake seconds later to my ribs snapping
One
     By

One
Opening boney doors
Releasing the separate quarters   of my heart
Lungs deflate
A wheeze catches   in my severed windpipe
I gasp
    Gasp
gasp
My spine departs from the tangle of skull
Snakes   away
Moist clacks across the floor
            My eyes are the last to leave the mess
Roll   away
Flopping awkwardly off to the dark
To   freedom

Stayed just long enough for me to see

I'm   revolting

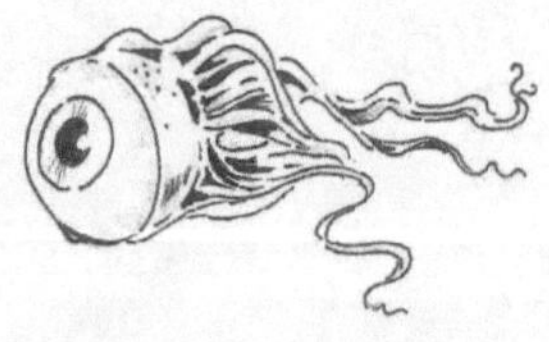

death and the butterfly

Death watched it drop
then softly land
upon his cold
and bony hand

Slowly spread
its wings apart
No trace of fear
there in its heart

"You know you live
a tiny life
Hardly worth
my time or strife

You'll live a week
or two at most
Simply just
a caterpillars ghost"

The butterfly raised
his tiny head
smiled up at Death
and then he said

"That's why I landed
 to say hello
You're out of place
 in this meadow

My time is short
and life is grand
Not my choice
but what's been planned

It's why I flitter
frantically
There's just so much
for me to see

The flowers blooming
every shade
dew left glistening
in the glade

I'll spend my hours
in the sun
until my time
on earth is done"

Then off he flew
into the sky
leaving Death
to ponder why

Something so small
so slight in size
should hold a thought
so vast and wise

His skull then cracked
his only smile
as he stared up
to the clouds awhile

His bones they clattered
to the ground
His robes fell next
without a sound

That shriveled, lost
and dusty part
That thing he once
had called a heart

Fluttered off
into the sun
His work he thought
was surely done

On the cosmos, then
His hand he'd stay
Untimely ends
he would delay

Cross time and space
this gift he'd give
A few more hours
in which to live

He'd leave his hourglass
on the shelf
and take a day then,
to himself

lonely waters

Lonely waters rush to shore
then retreat back to the deep once more

Icey tides caress the beach
Claiming all within her reach

Grasping at each stick and stone
Desperate not to feel alone

And when her longing grows too vast
Against the rocks her waves are cast

Lost in madness, ocean rages
Roaring waves sweep 'cross the ages

Can never then collect her fill
Her timeless heart lies empty still

Relentless need, it does not sleep
She rolls forever, black and deep

Never releases more than she saves
'Til the world again lies under the waves

You'll all be pulled into her breast
Your life, your love and all the rest

Avoid then the incoming tide
Her restless want she does not hide

The kelp it sways through still or storm
Seduction in its simplest form

Beware her lulling, tempting dirge
Ignore your all consuming urge

A death song born of froth and foam
Eternally sung, calling you home

Lonely waters pull you in
Never to be seen again

sinister sit the clowns

I see them there sitting
In the back corner
A single flickering bulb
Popping
Swaying in its metal shroud
Thick canvas tent flopping methodically in the breeze
Balloon uselessly bumping in the high shadows
Smells like hay
And things flies like

They're laughing
High and chittery
Like lunatics
But only men
Old and sad
Filthy
Dust caked in wrinkles where the grease paint flakes from
age
Torn, itchy trousers
Pale stains under their arms
Hair glistening on the backs of their necks
Their arms

Laughter stops when they see me
They stare
Silent in the stifling heat
Insects buzzing out in the sun
In the light

I step closer
Odor changes as I draw near
Earth after a hard rain
Something resembling worms

Breeze has stopped
Humidity rising
They stare

They are worse up close
Black webbing shows under patchy wigs
Stiff hair coming through like random fluorescent weeds
Pink gums run from stained teeth
Their nails unusually long
Red under them from applying their paint
But only red

The nearest one cocks his head
Questioning
A bell jingles somewhere

I tell him Mother left me at the fairgrounds
I tell him I saw her white dress once before the crowd
closed in
She was running
I tell him she was crying
He reaches over to an awkward stack of apple crates
Nails scrabbling

Searching
Powders fall like poison
Pretty

I'm sweating
It's so warm
He slides out a hand mirror
Small crack in the glass
With a grin he hands it to me

The chittering starts again
I bring the mirror to meet my
Sweat streaks down my face
revealing

White
yellow
And red.

And then I'm laughing as well

empty hearses

Empty hearses
Driving slow
Farewell my friend
cries the crow

Empty hearses
Gleaming black
Who's that cooling
in the back?

Empty hearses
Who has died?
Was it my father's
final ride?

Empty hearses
Did you send
my dear mother
to her end?

Empty hearses
Stale air
Dusty curtains
Silent prayer

Empty hearses
Heading home
Coming silent
and alone

Empty hearses
Gravel road
No longer burdened
by your load

Empty hearses
Setting sun
Empty hearses
What have you done?

the demon complacency

A demon whispers in my ear
things I think, but long to hear
"Life you know is just so tough
Never think you're not enough
Do your best that's all I ask
Surviving in itself's a task
You don't need them now, to approve
No need for you then to improve
No one else thinks much of you
No one will love you like I do"
So I sit and listen and agree
and watch my life just atrophy

I want to spend my ending days
Reading books down by the waves

Bird song floating on the breeze
Whales calling from the seas

Old chair sinking in the sand
Pages turned by shaking hand

The wind will whisper in my ear
Reminding me of all lost years

I'll read until my eyes grow dim
'Til next day then start again

And when my days are gone to past
My closing chapters read at last

No tear will fall to dampen page
Or give regret to ceasing age

I'll walk out far then past the shore
To rest my bones on the ocean floor

neighbors

There is a knocking
it's faint, but there
From up above
I'm not sure where

Soft at first
but growing strong
Not sure why
but something's wrong

Hear voices now
Whispers begin
A plea to my ears
saying "Let me in"

Footsteps sounding
their creaking tread
gently walking
overhead

A tapping then
from just outside
There's no escape
I cannot hide

My eyes are closed
My thoughts run free
What ghastly things
come torture me?

Insistent now
this constant drone
I beg of you,
"Leave me alone!"

This cannot be
These awful tones
The dreadful shrieks
The horrid moans

There's nails now
Sharp I fear
Dragging down
Drawing near

I'm screaming now
I clutch my sheet
I'm driven mad
My mind retreats

The noise above
at last has ceased
Perhaps now I
can rest in peace

The scratching stopped
but God forbid
an eye peers through
my coffin lid

  meet me in the flames

heartbeaten

Reach inside
Feel my heart
expanding
contracting
pushing out
pulling in
Is that where love lives?
I think not
Squeeze and you will see
Just a struggling muscle
blood
tissue
but in your grip
I'll still use my last breath
to say
I love you

To awaken
To the black
To the chill
My lungs spasm and inhale deeply, filling with stale, dead air.
I cough, quick and dry.
I am aware of the soft fluttering of my lids, irritated by some unknown dust.
As I go to clear my vision of this annoyance I notice a restriction, a hindrance of my arms beginning at the elbow and continuing to my shoulder as if I had found myself in the grip of some enormous, gloved hand compressing my limbs and in turn my very movement.
My head raised on my neck encounters similar resistance and I find my forehead grazing a silken surface, cold with a definite severity beneath.

And still the blackness.

My body I roll from side to side and feel this limitation at my hips as well as my knees, my limbs are confined to a slight motion of perhaps six inches at most and at this my heart lurches and I feel a dampness begin at my brow, a humidity to the stale air I am inhaling.
My fingers find the silk to my side, beneath me as above, they search blindly for some reference or sense of my predicament, finding only more silk and the occasional button

or seal. Beneath my trembling fingertips.
Frantic now, pressing my palms to the fabric above me I
push and scratch, feebly pounding as would an infant with
my limited mobility hearing only the dull thud of my fists
and the ever increasing beating of my own troubled heart.

And still the blackness

My head thrashes side to side imploring the void, willing
my eyes to focus
focus on something other than the nothingness surround-
ing me.
I feel the pressure now, in my temples, upon my chest,
intense unyielding pressure bearing down crushing me, flat-
tening my lungs and making my strangled breaths wheeze
from quivering lips.

Now the pillow my head was meant to rest upon is sodden
with my rank sweat turned even more foul in these close
confines. My breath erratic taking in panicked gulps of
thickening air, staler for the reuse of it.

Dear god ….

Dear god!!!

I'm clawing at my shrouding, tearing the cloth in a hopeless
frenzy
shredding it
Fingers scrabble against the metal underneath sending des-
perate echoes down toward my feet and back again.
My nails break in the effort and I flinch at the hot droplets
pattering onto my face, I blink to the darkness but the pain
is lost to the utter panic of this unholy occurrence.

I …

I think of the dirt above me, cold, compacted, immovable
and dense, full of stone and root and foul with crawling,
inching, grubbing things.
Making their slow, determined descent

My breath catches in my chest, a sob building and tears run
burning from my eyes, down round my cheeks, gone to the
silk
A shrill chuckle jumps from my mouth, sanities last stran-
gled gasp
Torturous thoughts roll backward
Delicate tethers of self stretch and snap
My mind is lost to me
I sense it spilling out of my skull, tumbling back into black
caverns
And I scream…
To the dark
To the unforgiving earth
To the omni present worm
I scream
I scream
I scream

the resurrection man

Come along and take my hand
Come and meet the Resurrection Man

You've lost someone too much to bear?
Forsaken your holy book of prayer?

Your soul is aching, all is lost
Your heart needs mending, damn the cost

Go to him when all else fails
You'll find him in his coat and tails

"Come sit down child, speak your woes
Tell me your troubles, see how it goes"

"I'll give those bones a second chance
I'll bring dead grandma back to dance"

Then on his knees he begins to pray
Round and round he starts to sway

Chanting in some backward tongue
He bids them back to which they've come

He'll spin around and spit and curse
Just drop some coins into his purse

Eyes roll back he starts to foam
As he brings your loved one home

They need to be fresh for the connection to hold
Not enough times can this rule be told

Under three days buried in tombs
Or floating blue, still stiff in the womb

No bodies that squish or covered in mold
He can do nothing when they've gotten that old

They return to you sure but not quite the same
Might be your dear mother, but only in name

Silent and still they speak not a word
At least not a word that's ever been heard

They sit and they stare at night to the stars
You can't make that journey without taking some scars

Some can't cope, they put them back in the dirt
Others adapt, need a balm for the hurt

So if still you find yourself, determined and bound
your true love has recently been put in the ground

Square up your shoulders and straighten your back
Stuff sainted papa in an old gunny sack

Drag him on down to that dead end street
Where the line between life and eternity meet

Come on darlin' take my hand
It's time you meet the Resurrection Man

blackbird, blackbird

Blackbird, blackbird
Hear me cry
take me with you to the sky

Blackbird, blackbird
Hear me pray
for this be my dying day

Blackbird, blackbird
Leave my bones
to molder there amongst the stone

Blackbird, blackbird
Hear my plea
Let's fly out now past the sea

Blackbird, blackbird
Hear me wail
A life of beak and wing and tail

Blackbird, blackbird
Hear me urge
sing me now my final dirge

Blackbird, blackbird
Take my soul
my love already you have stole

This where I take your hand
Pull you off the ground
Dust you off, lead you away
You utter not a sound

This is where I take your breath
Directly from your lungs
In desperate, panting gasps
From you, my name is sung

This is where I take your eyes
I am all that they behold
Trust only what I show you
Not the lies that you've been told

This is where I take your heart
Each fearful, frantic beat
A weak and foolish thing you hold
Lay the offering at my feet

This is where I take your mind
Every thought you've ever known
Smile at me, somewhat vacantly
thoughts no longer yours alone

This is where I eat you whole
Who you were? No one can ever tell
No deep sighs or teary eyes
You wished for this as well

unturned

In my mouth
sits your tongue
so I can taste your truth

In my hands
lie your eyes
so I can learn your proof

In your heart
sticks the blade
I buried there today

In my arms
lies your corpse
a cold and pallid gray

In my ears
I hear the screams
of lessons left unlearned

Vile things live under rocks
Some stones....
are better left unturned

my salvation

My salvation
Wears an ancient,
blood red cloak
Walks in flame,
He's ringed in smoke

My salvation
Comes on my
most darkest nights
Beneath his wings,
he holds me tight

My salvation
Whispers lies,
I do not mind
Most truth is lies,
I've come to find

My salvation
Does not command me
bend and kneel
A single kiss,
his promise sealed

My salvation
No need for names then,
on a list
Unlike yours,
he does exist

A greasy sweat breaks
Cold
I should feel better by now
My stomach cramps
I fall to my knees
I vaguely remember
in the heat
my fingers in my mouth

This is why we wear gloves

chills

I wish I wasn't alone
but I am
but I'm not

a friend in need

I saw the devil and he looked tired
so together we walked for awhile
arm in arm through the ruins
and spoke of things most vile

His voice like tainted honey
dripped warmly in my ear
I'm sick of death and despair he said
From his eye fell a single tear

Eons spent in exile
surrounded by death and decay
The worst that humanity can offer
flooding in day after day

'Twas time my mere mention
would still the hearts of man
I was the black, the deep, the silence
A cold shadow since time began

You come to me now in legion
far many for my minions to bear
'Tis not your numbers which vex me
but the smiles on the faces you wear

The relief in your eyes as you enter
quite plainly for me 'tis to tell
There is nothing that I can do lately
which is worse than you do to yourselves

The endless struggle for power
Wars waged solely on greed
Fear and despair and corruption
Mothers milk on which you feed

He bowed his horned head just then
and fell to a quivering knee
I feel my time of purpose has passed
Now sadly I just long to be free

I took his downcast chin in hand
and raised his eyes to mine
"Do not despair," I said to him
"We all need a friend time to time"

They need you on your throne of bones
dark lord of the stygian pit
We need to know through darkest dreams
in Hell you'll forever sit

For if the cauldrons were to turn cold
and the fires finally put out
Nothing would bind the souls of man
if your existence were truly in doubt

So rise up now, reclaim your realm
Your unholy vows renew
Fill your black heart with what passes for hope
for I still believe in you

He brushed the dust then from his coat
ran claws through his silky, black hair
Looked back just once, gave me a grin
turned and descended the stairs

 meet me in the flames

if i were blind

If I were blind
I'd write you a note
No tears to fall on the page
No ink do I need
Somehow, I've been freed
As if sight were a restricting cage

If I were blind
I'd write you a poem
Of all we have yet to be
No use are my eyes
With their devious lies
Sometimes you need darkness to see

If I were blind
I'd write you a song
To tell you what love's all about
No light would I use
The dark be my muse
For that's where the truth comes out

beneath the mask, i wait

I see you
through the holes I've pulled
The terror
I smell you
The fear
rank
stinging
I'm right here
see me
hidden
always
hidden
I feel you
I taste you
through HIS makeshift mouth
into mine

I'm here
right behind
hidden
I feel sweat around my eyes
stinging
Behind my ears
I smell fabric
thick and dry
sour
My nose drips

There are fibers in my mouth
I leave them
they are a part of HIM
I look out through ragged slits
hidden
He speaks for me
Covers me
Protects me
I still smell fear

HE is me
I am you

Victims

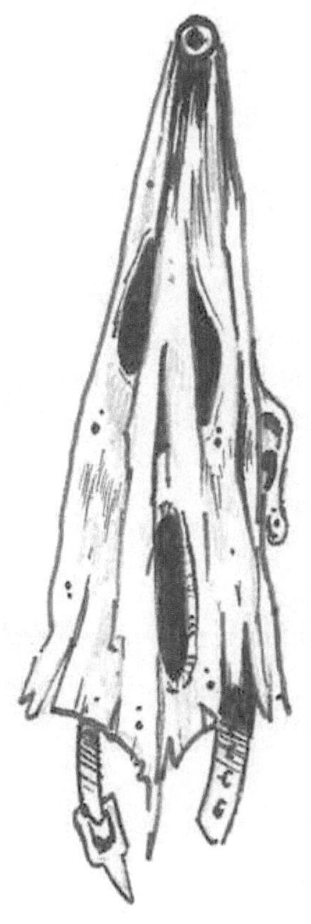

Meet me in the flames
My Lord
Meet me in the flames
They broke my body on the rack
To your arms I stumble back
Meet me in the flames

Whisper from the fire
My Lord
Whisper from the fire
Tell me now, over my cries
Of eternal love and all other lies
Whisper from the fire

Hold me as we burn
My Lord
Hold me as we burn
My lungs hold water from the creek
Take me now, my knees grow weak
Hold me as we burn

Find me in the coals
My Lord
Find me in the coals
Seek me out, I cannot see
The rats they took my eyes from me
Find me in the coals

Kiss me in the ash
My Lord
Kiss me in the ash
Let me be your blackest bride
Across the moon tonight I ride
Kiss me in the ash

He said she had lifeless eyes
A doll's eyes.
Then she moved past me
and that eye passed over
and it was black
and it was cold
and it was ancient
and time paused as she appraised me
majestically indifferent
graceful
exquisite
Until I saw her teeth

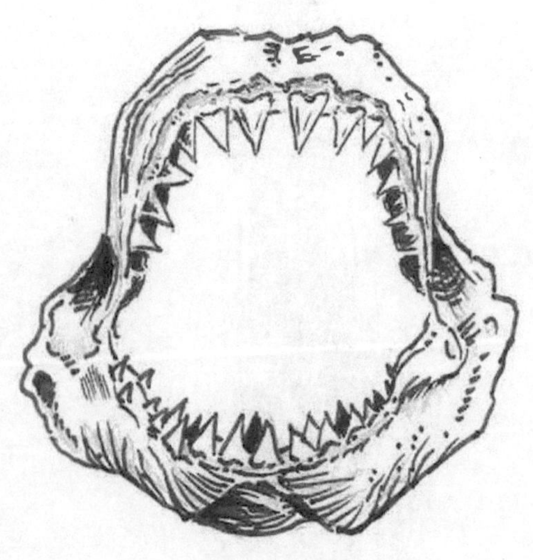

tasting of abandonments

I found her
livid
clouds rolled through her gray eyes
Sadness in the way her lips parted
Framing a word
I knelt down in the weeds
Brushed a damp hair from her eyes
and kissed her
She tasted of abandonments
and words she never spoke

the loneliness of autumn

On the cold October breeze
drift the dead and brittle leaves

Overseeing from his cross
damp and torn and flecked with moss

The scarecrow stares from lonely perch
Pastor in a dying church

Stuffed with straw a ragged shirt
Hung from a pole stuck in the dirt

Keeping counsel with the crows
holding silent secrets told

No field mouse or bird come near
Tiny hearts hold mostly fear

Left alone to sag and rot
A single friend is all he sought

Pleading to the swaying husks
From rising sun to fading dusk

Send me someone to converse
Free me from this lonesome curse

  meet me in the flames

Through many sad and desperate years
Begging that someone appear

Then from the rustling stalks of corn
Something wicked has been born

Up from the ground past root and seed
It craves despair on which to feed

This scarecrow's desperate, hopeless chest
The perfect place in which to nest

Up the pole it slowly drags
Its ancient form up through the rags

Scarecrow shudders in the breeze
At last, an answer to his pleas

He's given host to something old
And deeper than December cold

Bringing tales from beneath
Tales of suffering and of grief

For endless hours recounting pain
How many horrors can one contain?

The scarecrow cries for none to hear
The fabric soaks up every tear

What beast is this that heard his call?
What evil through his heart now crawls?

Burlap sack with holes for eyes

Behind them heaven knows what lies

So when the corn whips in the fields
Wind blows hard, sorrows revealed

His head hangs lowest on those nights
tortured by forbidden sights

If you happen by this place
The moonlight shining on his face

Might turn his tattered head your way
Look down at you as if to say,

"Unto the grain don't offer prayers
Best be alone than suffer terrors"

You might wonder then, as you walk past
Recalling eyes so deep and vast

What mysteries then does he retain
Those many midnights in the rain?

confessions

Bless me Father for I have sinned
My last confession was 8 days ago
I'm locked inside a silent scream
I've cut myself again it seems

Grows hard to keep the poison in
It calls to me under my skin

Bless me Father for I have sinned
My last confession was 6 days ago
I cannot eat. I do not sleep
Like Christ my wounds are left to weep

Your voice is soothing to the ear
but not the only one I hear

Bless me father for I have sinned
My last confession was 2 days ago
Things I fear have grown much worse
Though I toil with bead and verse

My knife is dull from overuse
My flesh grows weak from the abuse

Bless me father for I have sinned
I confessed to you but yesterday
I suffer with the constant bray
Demands for pain both night and day

greg jones -71-

His word I read 'til lids go slack
They laugh and curse and spit them back

Bless me Father for I have sinned
My last confession was but this morn
The voices whisper and seduce
The prayers you give me are no use

There is no hope for me I fear
My ears removed but still I hear

Bless me Father? I have no need
My last confession has been heard
I sense the fear within your voice
You still believe I have a choice?

The cuttings stopped, I am to heal
To older gods I'm bound to kneel

Forgive me Father you have been kind
I stand before you as assigned
At last, I have no more to tell
The voice demands the priest as well

the goats in the barn

Papa come see the goats in the barn
Papa come see the goats in the barn
I braided their tails with thistles and yarn
Papa come see the goats in the barn

On hind legs they dance round and round
On hind legs they dance round and round
Clacking their hooves as the bells softly sound
On hind legs they dance round and round

Mother come look at the goats in their stalls
Mother come look at the goats in their stalls
They all come a runnin' when the black one he calls
Mother come look at the goats in their stalls

Their fur is all matted and covered in flies
Their fur is all matted and covered in flies
They stare at each other and whisper their lies
Their fur is all matted and covered in flies

Brother come look at the goats in their pens
Brother come look at the goats in their pens
Neath their fur lies a symbol of a time before men
Brother come look at the goats in their pens

They wear my black dresses with buckles and lace
They wear my black dresses with buckles and lace
Of kindness their dark eyes betray not a trace
They wear my black dresses with buckles and lace

Sister come see the goats while they dance
Sister come see the goats while they dance
For your the last one to come have a glance
Sister come see the goats while they dance

They all hang from beams eight feet off the ground
They all hang from beams eight feet off the ground
The goats and I gone, nowhere to be found
They all hang from beams eight feet off the ground

as through gauze

Stiff lids
Massive
Gummed shut
Opening
Slowly
Eyes roll forward
Focus
Slowly
Red shadows
Blood ghosts
Pain behind
Shards
Thin shards
Black glass
Tugging
Cutting
Cool blue
Light
White
I blink
Pink
Pain again
The ghosts dissipate
Reform
Clearer
Dissolve

Reform
Clearer
See
Understand
first time
See
The truth
Close my eyes

I long for ghosts

reawakening

The heavy door slowly swinging open
The squeal of the hinges in the silence
The tinking flicker of the fluorescents
The drawer standing empty
The scratch marks on the inside panel
The biting smell of sterilization
The moisture fading from the steel tray
The footsteps leading out the door
The toe tag crumpled in the trash

long pig

A missionary came to my village one day
Curious to hear to which gods we prayed

He was polite and well mannered, a genuine chap
He listened most intently with his hands in his lap

The elder then spoke of the god in the ground
Who made meager seeds into rations abound

Of the god of the sky who brings forth the rain
To sooth our dry throats and water our grain

The volcano god with his terrible wraith
Appeased only with virgins who have been cut in half

At this the priest appeared quite green
Obviously this was something he'd never seen

The jungle god, said the shaman, not missing a beat
Steals our children at night on soft, padded feet

And finally, the fertility god he said with a wink
A favorite of his, I soon came to think

The priest then rose, kissed his cross and he said
Let me tell you of MY god and from his book he then read

The tale he told of the man and his cross
Of his betrayal and death and life of such loss

There were women and snakes and a man in a whale
A man come from dust, from his rib a female

Six days of work and one day of rest?
In the jungle, that would not work out for the best

We looked at each other round the fire that night
All hiding glances and grins hard to fight

He went on and on with passion and poise
Speaking most directly to the young girls and boys

Jesus will save you, each woman and man
It was then that the shaman held up his own hand

Be done with your preaching! He yelled with a roar
What kind of fools do you take us for?

A man who spreads water so his people may pass?
Although… flesh of my body and my blood in a glass…

These tales are foolish and no good to us here
Out the tent he was ushered at the point of a spear

Out came the whole tribe and they all gathered round
As the preacher was forced to his knees on the ground

It was then that he noticed their sharp little teeth
The part in their loin cloths and what lay beneath

Crusty old bone knives still sharp he was sure
With bits of hair hanging from what came before

The shaman then whispered in the ear of the priest
I forgot to mention the god of the feast

With a panther's black talon he began to cut
Opening him up from apple to nut

We danced and we screamed and we painted our eyes
With the blood of the priest our most holy prize

His guts gathered up and then put to a boil
Scooping tiny bits up from the dark jungle soil

We picked clean his bones, threw them into a pile
Let the children and dogs enjoy him awhile

All that was left of the man when we'd fed
Were some dusty old beads and the book he had read

Many others have tried over the years to convert
Bring us this Jesus with his guilt and his hurt

We give thanks to the sky and the gods we pray toward
Our bellies grow fat on the word of their Lord.

The sun hangs heavy just over the tree line
Darkness rising
I make my way through dead grass
stiff
Past things gone to rust
The house is shifted
Leans to one side
a crippled relative
Porch boards sag under my weight
deficient
"Hello," I call
Screen door screams on its hinge,
bangs closed behind me
"Hello" again
Nothing
Just warm silence
Feel a presence
Pass into the drawing room
Silence
Filthy light weakly leaks in
Figures
Standing, sitting, crouching
Water sits thick in the glass
A fly on the lip
Infant sucks lazily on a heavy breast
The milk
It smells yellow

Eyes adjust to the gloom
more figures in the half light
They rise
approach
Slack lips press my skin
Smiles lacking teeth
Heavy, stale breath
my hand in a toddler's mouth
He presses down with affection
Like a pup
I pull back
My hand tinged in pink
Old fingers in my hair
Down my face
I'm touched
Caressed
Misshapen hands paw at me
The sun sinks below the trees
Something surrenders in my chest
The tears come hot

Family can be such a comfort at times.

sarah at dawn

Sarah watched her
put the broomstick between her legs,
grip,
then rise.
She absently touched the swelling under her eye
and with a half smile
watched her disappear over the tree line
with an equal measure of terror
and envy.

becoming the wolf

Bright full moon
Damp forest ground
Circle been scratched
Eight feet round

Skin is chilled
By midnight mist
Stand here naked
Slice my wrist

Lamb in sack
Cut her throat
Blood flows freely
Down her coat

Mix our blood
Herb and spice
Speak the name
Once then twice

Skin of wolf
Round my waist
Blood of lamb
Then I taste

Spread the gore
For my birth

Lie down now
Upon the earth

Prayers in silence
White moons glow
Feel the change
Begin to show

Hot drool spills
Skin does twitch
In my mouth
Teeth do itch

Eyes roll up
Turn to white
Then roll back
To other sight

Nails turn black
Sharp as knives
Long for taking
Of their lives

Hear bones pop
And muscles stretch
Hair like bristles
Cross my chest

My first howl
Bay at moon
The final veil
Will fall soon

Strength in limbs
Has now grown
A hunger like
I've never known

Now I race
Past the wood
Fire in hearth
Flee they should

Growl with rage
Break the door
Eat their flesh
Man no more

Please don't let me see
all that will never be
The paths that lay uncrossed,
all the lovers lost
on my way cross the bottomless sea

Please don't let me hear
our song come cross my ear
Calling from the shore
words I'll hear no more
as cold eternity draws near

Please don't let me feel
our secret truths revealed
As my dust is blown
from all I've ever known,
my fate upon the earth forever sealed

Please just let me know
as I begin to row
I'll sometimes cross the minds
of those I leave behind
and to the red horizon I will go.

David

He came here
He touched me
His hands….
His fingers were….
bleeding
David, he said he knew you
He envied you
wanted to be you

I told him about the baby
I told him.
But never told you
I told this monster a secret I hadn't told the man I love
I tried to save us
I'm sorry
I'm so sorry

David
I'm here
It's dark in the box, David
I'm in the box

I'm in the box
Don't wake up, David
Don't wake up

It rains here all the time

  meet me in the flames

She came to me then in my bunker
Pushed past my lips as I slept
Secreting her seed
To resist was no need
For eons their patience they kept

So this then is how it begins
with a silent surrender of skin
The egg sacs that coat
the walls of my throat
have burst from the pressure within

New children come forth by the thousands
flooding my mouth in erratic waves
Out from me they pour
slick with my gore
It's the light of a new world they crave

They cascade down a feverish body
frantically scratching my now naked skin
Around me they weave
and my mind does not grieve
but welcomes the changes within

Encased in this gossamer coffin
through webs pass my last human breath
My chrysalis complete
the little ones retreat
to await my inevitable death

The fine hairs cross my body start growing
I'm alive with a sensory joy
Then my body it splits
as out through the slits
eight legs which I can now employ

My abdomen engorges quite slowly
to three times its average size
On my beauty I gaze
through the thin milky glaze
of my newly formed multiple eyes

Fangs push through a discarded face
twitching with eager intent
Poison fills my glands
I sense them expand
Glorious pain, it will not relent

My children they watch from the dust
In each shadowed corner of the room
No hint of fear lies
In their unblinking eyes
As I shriek from my delicate womb

This hunger it burns like a flame
I long to digest my first kill
Once my prey is selected
The venom injected

  meet me in the flames

I can drink 'til my stomachs they fill

At last, I am free from the prison
Twitching, I fall moist to the floor
I hoist my new girth
Awash in rebirth
Delighted to be human no more

Out into the new dawn we rise
It is my time and soon I must mate
The last one lies dead
To my children was fed
There's a dead earth to repopulate

the sad man

We sat on the ledge
the sad man and I
and watched the gray clouds
as they crawled through the sky

He had tears in his eyes
as he spoke out at last
No hope for the future
No love for his past

He raised his head
and said with a sigh
"All my days are spent lately
just wondering why"

"There are no answers
Nothing's for sure
Just a bleak uncertainty
for which there's no cure"

He put his head in his hands
and started to weep
Then I broke the one promise
I swore I would keep

I whispered a secret
deep into his ear
A secret he knew
but just needed to hear

A slow, knowing nod
for now answers he had
and now the sad man
was no longer sad

He smiled just then
and with a wink of his eye
Put his best foot forward
and stepped into the sky

No one saw me
for I wasn't there
Just his voice on the wind
like an unanswered prayer

Beware the black lake
the withered ones say
With white, rheumy eyes
they look to the skies
and in hushed tones, softly they pray

Tales are told of this bleak, evil lake
No birdsong or insect to hear
A dead wind in the trees
Nothing scurries through leaves
It is a place to avoid and to fear

Her surface remains as still as the glass
No ripple or wake ever show
Silent and cold
Prehistorically old
as the ones who lie slumbering below

For in that ancient, glacial lake
a presence there always has been
Under warped, tangled roots
before sandals and boots
of even the earliest men

Her bed of muck lies littered with bones
Beneath silt from centuries past
and a gray, choking fog
rises up from the bog
each night when the moon falls at last

The trees round her banks grow twisted with rot
Their limbs all point down toward the deep
Carved neath their bark
hidden from all but the dark,
the ghastly, black language they speak

If you listen close in the time before dawn
You'll hear a soft chant, like a hymn
Drawing you down
through the weeds 'til you drown
not a bubble to betray where you'd been

A song you will hear, low and deep
but nothing your ears can discern
It's felt in your bones
those unholy tones
and for her black waters you'll yearn

So if from the banks you're caught staring
deeply as if in a mirror
No face you'll detect
for she does not reflect
Only death staring back, drawing near

It's then that your soul will be gone
lost to the shores of this place
From that low pulsing hum
she beckons you come

greg jones   -95-

Resistance there is not a trace

From your throat a scream silent and long
sanity claimed by your cries
It's black, rotted lines
unmoored from your mind
as lake water leaks from your eyes

For in madness only, may your voice
be added to the chorus below
Then with unsteady steps
you pass through the depths
and into her cold arms you will go

the language of hunger

Hear them calling in the dark
near
strangled, desperate cries
just outside
my dying fire
The sound of emptiness
The language of hunger
I hear my heart
also desperate
thrashing and banging in its cage
and I wonder at the words
it will scream
when I'm opened
and left to cool in the frost

mourning doll

Mourning doll
Mourning doll
Same as my love
Rest your head on her pillow
She looks down from above

Mourning doll
Mourning doll
Face milky as cream
Your presence here now
Allows me to dream

Mourning doll
Mourning doll
Your lacy white dress
She wore only once
On the day she was blessed

Mourning doll
Mourning doll
So precious and fair
Beneath the veil adorned
With my darling's own hair

Mourning doll
Mourning doll
I visit each morn
Peering into your crib
Like the day you were born

Mourning doll
Mourning doll
Still praying for when
I'll hear your sweet voice
and your eyes open again

Mourning doll
Mourning doll
My tears will not cease
I hope that your nearness
Will grant me some peace

Mourning doll
Mourning doll
She's not really gone
In chill winds, she returns
Through your eyes she looks on

caress of the rat queen

My body
My blood
which I give up to you
I sacrifice
Take me
Burrow in
Gnaw me
in pieces
I feel your teeth on my bones
Feel you writhing
Boiling in my cavity
Hear your greasy squealing
The cry of your thousand offspring
Take my offerings
Carry me off
to your young
I nourish
Feed off me
I'm barren
Hollow me
coring
You're my new heart
Slick with your oils
Pulsing
Seething
You worm and uncurl
Squirming

Your heat warms me
The heat of your couplings
Your fleas dance
In recesses
In sockets
Taking my blood
leaving their seed
They call us vermin

They call us filth
Ripening occurs in the dirt
In the dark
things grow

You're carrying me off
Aloft on a hundred tiny backs
Your tails twitch under me

Off
to the unlit place
toward the damp
Praise be

All miracles are first denied

nest in me

Our love was left
in an airless room
of an empty house,
our husks
crumbling,
tumbling across the floor
Hollow hands reach
but never touch

like always

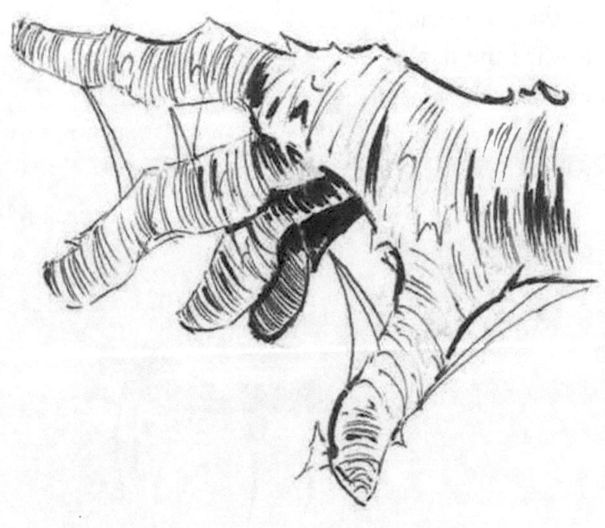

christopher

Did the shadows of my room just grow darker?
It's midnight but I swear I did see
Past the foot of my bed,
the slow turn of a head
Now it's peering directly at me

From the corner it's red eyes glow
Embers of some hellish flame
Falling under its gaze
in some thick, foggy haze
I fear that my soul it will claim

I hear it there in the dark breathing
A raspy, wet, rattling wheeze
Then from its black form
dreadful sounds, weakly born
like the moan of some dead, creaking trees

As if from the grave the stench hits me
My stomach a slow, rancid roll
The smell of its breath
thick with past death
The terror now taking its toll

My fingers like iron grip my heart

Pounding so hard as to burst
From my chest the sharp pains
ice water in veins
"Be gone foul demon," I curse

It lurches closer now, this devil
Moonlight betraying its frame
then rising up high
lets out a low sigh
and softly it whispers my name

Hot urine it comes
my terrified bladder drains bare
for my mind stands no more
of the sheer, utter horror
at the sight of what's now standing there

A cold, taloned hand
to my throat tightly grabs hold
Dripping fangs have appeared
its mouth drawing near
Leather wings begin to unfold

My head is pulled back
as its lustful feeding begins
Eyes flutter closed
in my deathly throes
but then find themselves open again

I wake and cry out to the screen
"Damn you, Christopher Lee!!!"
Up half the night
bathed in the light
of your movies on late night TV.

  meet me in the flames

false flesh

My dresses never fit
They itched and bunched
false skins
My parents would rage
Turn my world from pink
to red
The skins made to fit
however possible
I've grown accustomed
I see myself in them
Them in me
Soon my son will be born
from the gash I have made
between my legs
And I will love him
as I have been loved
brutally
and in utter darkness

fear adds the flavor

My fingers are sticky
thick
gritty
I lick them clean
Sure to get the gobs under my nails
I dig something from a rotted tooth
just a small knuckle
I suck the grist and spit it across the cave
air harsh with burnt hair
I try to pluck them the best I can
That's why the babies are best
Time to turn the spit
Some I leave to crisp until the tiny bones break
The marrow hot in my throat
soothes my pain
warms my bones
Something whimpers in a far corner
Good
Fear adds the flavor
My sisters told me to enjoy my youth
I cackle and take another bite
I'm feeling younger already

kristina

Who hung the swing in the graveyard
from the dead tree by the far northern wall?
It gently starts swaying come midnight
and continues 'til the moon makes it fall

The old wooden plank, it lies empty
as the rope passes over her bones
Not a hint is detected come daybreak
but the footprints encircling her stone

Listen close in the time before sunrise
when the stars back to heaven are bid
For the soft lilting tone of her laughter
and the slow creaking close of the lid

the attention of the fly

I've caught the attention of the fly,
beloved filth
I welcome her,
her erratic dance
She rubs her hands together
Eager
Ravenous
A thousand eyes survey me
Thousands,
upon thousands
I am her mosaic
Her head tilts
She's found her spot
Then
Her caustic kiss
Probing
Corroding me
Opening me
A sensual destruction
Others follow,
on my scent
They find my openings
Wounds
Tear ducts
A chapped lip
Their tongues assaulting me,
dissolving me

 meet me in the flames

Me
The surrogate
Why do I enjoy this?
Am I dead inside?
Now I wait
for conception
My larval stage
I'm beaming
Like all mothers
Maggots teeming
I throb with new life
Millions
I hear their consumption
deep in my ears
Their insistence
The scritch of their indulgence
I burst
I collapse
I succumb
I am leaking life
They cascade from me in curtains
I vomit from a dozen mouths
They fall from me like a pale rain
Wriggle blindly on the ground
Some taken alight
Sparrows and wrens feeding their young
Some are set upon by those who slither,
who scurry
Some born to flies themselves
All carry a taste of me
I live on
in a million tiny ways

what remains

———

When all is done and all been said
The beasts have all, at last, been fed

Your flesh been measured out in pound
Just tattered scraps left to be found

Bones now ground beneath the wheel
No more days under their heel

You've lived your life, you've drunk your fill
Ran the tab and paid the bill

Stood your ground and shook your fist
Crossed each item off your list

If in your chest your heart is true
Doubtful beats have been kept few

No one else's thoughts hold sway
You've lived your life your own way

Doesn't matter who they see
What they wanted you to be

Their biased, plain and basic views
Faded, worn out thoughts of you

You've given all you've had to share
Love the man left lying there

When you're left staring out to space
Recalling date and time and place

Faces hover just above
Eyes downcast, but full of love

So when you finally breathe your last
Through smiling lips let breath be past

Your final whisper here on earth
A testament to all you're worth

Bless their ears with something wise
Before you slowly close your eyes

Leave skeptics circling overhead
There is no shame left to the dead

They'll scratch and search what's left behind
For any dirt that they might find

Simple minds dwell on the stains
The truth you lived is what remains

it's all in your head

Look down the hallway
Check under the bed
Stop jumping at shadows
It's all in your head

The creak on the stairway?
That noise overhead?
That voice that I hear?
It's all in your head

It visits each night
This feeling of dread
Find it hard to believe
It's all in my head

My eyes will not close
They're bloodshot and red
I just stare in the darkness
It's all in your head

I'm desperate for sleep
nerves beginning to shred
This cannot go on
It's all in your head

Just take this prescription
The doctors had said
These symptoms will fade
It's all in your head

They're treatments have failed
Just lies I've been fed
It's just mild delusions
It's all in your head

I try to escape
But just lie here instead
Too frightened to move
It's all in your head

Ghosts are not real
You can't see the dead
She's still buried out back
It's all in your head

But she's lying beside me
Damp on the spread
That smell of the grave?
It's all in your head

Right here on my chest
she places her head
Is that a smile I see?
It's all in your head

Her throat is all ragged
And stained where she bled
I had to be certain

It was all in my head

She lays her cold hand
The hand I had wed
Across my eyes and she whispers
"It's all in your head"

Then she shows me a vision
Of what lies ahead
I just keep telling myself
It's all in your head

the wolf parade

The wolf parade, it files past
Upon me yellow eyes are cast

On my bones will not devour
Save that for another hour

On hind legs they strut and prance
Once a year they get this chance

To set aside their hunger pangs
Cease the hunt and blunt the fangs

Come out from shadows, black and cold
Live not in fear, but brash and bold

Moon shines down, it's high and bright
Wolves all howl as one this night

Cold and barefoot from my bed
To this place to which I've fled

I'll search for things I sorely lack
Nestled there within the pack

Oh to run and chase, to hunt and sing
Find awe in what the new day brings

So throw me to the wolves I say
Cloak me in a coat of gray

May I join you brother, hand in hand?
Leave behind this world of man?

Turn my back, lock all my doors
Morning finds me on all fours

rolling the deep

I feel like I'm floating
weightless
She takes me in her mouth
pulls me in
Deep
Deeper
I feel a pressure in my groin
across my stomach
We're rolling
rolling
I'm delirious
I'm wrapped around her
My head is spinning
I reach for her
My hands on her face
Fingers in her mouth
She is fierce
She has me shaken
shattered
I'm coming apart
then the release
I'm floating again
away
Slowly she blinks
Glides off
We're not finished
She'll be back
to take the rest of me

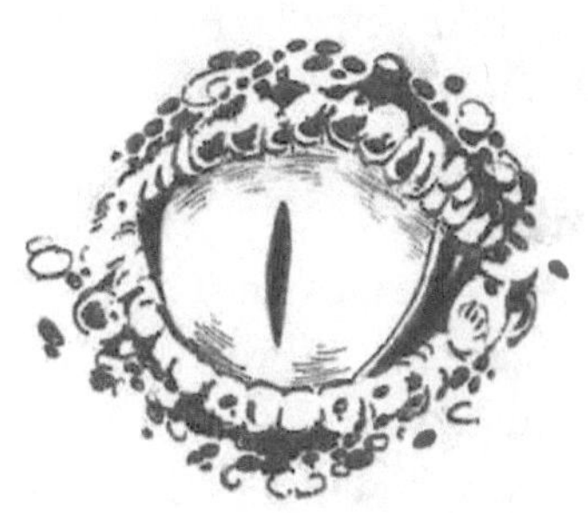

the rectory

I walk into the rectory
always with a hint of shame
unworthiness
It's silent
An overly warm air hangs
oppressive
thick in my lungs
plush carpet smothering my footsteps

Take in the shelves and bookcases and filing cabinets
and think
what are all these binders?
Are there actually user manuals for God?
Divine instruction?
Holy how-tos?
I smile
If so the pages must all be blank

Outdated photos frame on the walls
Faded yellow smiles coming through the dusty glass
eerie in the half light
I feel watched
There are heavy, woolen secrets here
I imagine the uncomfort of sitting there
crossing and uncrossing legs
upholstery stained with the sweat of past sinners
I sympathize

His office door is ajar
I step in
A bit cooler in here but not much
An old oscillating fan off somewhere, whirs

Dark oak absorbs the scant light filtering in through the
dingy curtains
More faded photos
more yellowed smiles
more leering, half-open eyes
on me
There is a file on the desk
under the lamp
I open it

I was wrong about the blank pages
Some pages have names listed
Some of those names are crossed out

names like mine

She opened her mouth
Rolled her tongue back
The symbols shone wetly
"Kiss me"
So I did
And, in the blood, we created a new language
Her
with her tongue of ink
Me
with my teeth
filed to a point
sharp as pen nibs

dinner for two

My eyes roam over you before me
The table has been set for two
Wine is poured, the silver is laid
Tonight it's just me and you

Flowers throughout the banquet
Their fragrance hangs thick in the air
Beauty my love, all around us
But nothing compared to you lying there

I'll eagerly sample each morsel
Bring bites to my quivering lips
Slice gently through skin and through muscle
Cut you dear into flavorful strips

Meat glistens moist under candlelight
Deep hues of pink and of red
Mouth full of your savory beauty
Fingertips stained where you bled

Your juice runs warm down my gullet
My tongue throbs with impatient glee
I could bury my face in your goodness
Gorge on you like a shark out at sea

A portion removed from your bicep
Just a taste of your succulent thigh
A delicacy are each of your eyelids
Followed up, of course, by your eyes

Save your tenderest parts for the last
Eat them raw, the purist of taste
Slide down the throat like an oyster
We'll let nothing of you go to waste

Wipe my mouth with a fine linen napkin
Push my chair in a gentleman's way
Kiss you where your lips once lie pouted
Close the cooler, that's enough for today

r i c t u s

What brings a smile to your face?
In that black and airless space

What do your empty eyes behold?
As you gaze out to the cold

Some knowledge we already know
A secret whispered down below?

We all wear the same black grin
Right below our failing skin

It plays across our drying bones
Unveiled to the sticks and stones

What brings to you that mirthful s
Among the dark and silent dirt

Keep your deceits and all your lies
Tell your falsehoods to the flies

We all soon view the final proof
Trudging slowly toward the truth

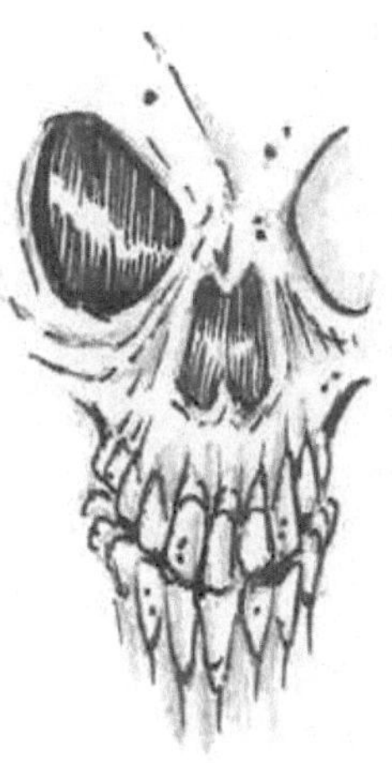

Do you feel far off eyes on you
Their cruel intentions
Their entitled desires
Their teeth slick from the unconscious roving of tongues
Lips thick
white paste rims the corners of their mouths
they are watching you flee and stumble and scream
They love it
They crack their knuckles and pursue
Through the forest
Through the streets
Through the clubs
The dating sites
The lecture halls
They look to each other for permission to laugh and it's
granted
Always
They run on legs built for this
The hunt
They toss giggles to the dusk
Like jackals
Tongues lolling
Panting
The dust swirls
Heat shimmers
And the strongest or quickest or shrewdest of them carries

you off
Limp
Helpless
You stare out
Lose yourself
For yourself
Sacredly guarding what's left
If anything

Boys are the worst

to bite

Fine hairs pass softly over your tongue
Nostrils flare open taking in the heady scent
Pungent
So…
Human
A hot spill of drool runs from the corner of your mouth
Unbidden
But not necessarily…
Unwanted
There is an…
Itch
In your teeth
A dull ache
A want
You know what lies just beneath
Running
Pulsing
So you bring it into your mouth
Tentative at first
Uncertain
Then taking more
Gagging softly
But you don't stop
No
You press
Down

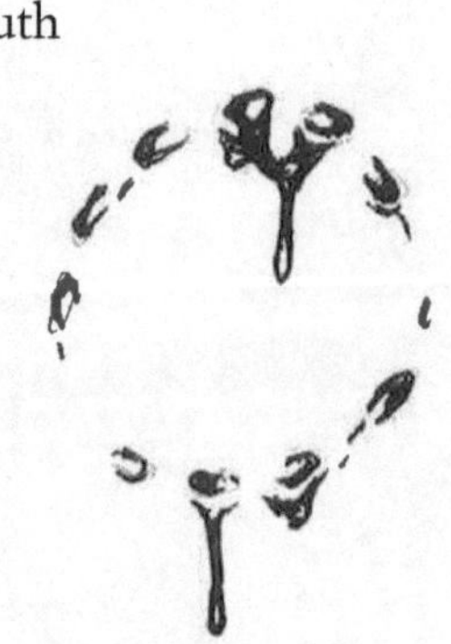

Just slightly
And you're aware now
Aware of what your lips are touching
Aware of the soft movement of your tongue in your
mouth
Readying itself
Eager
You press further
Feel the tissues slight opposition
The skin's resistance to its fate
Its disbelief
Emboldened you press
Still the muscle holds
And the drool spills freely
And your jaws twitch
And they yearn
Impatient with this seduction
The audacity of the flesh
To refuse
Then your teeth are pushing through
Joining in the redness
The meat gives
Your mind registers in that instant
And questions
Will this moment be glorious?
Will it be unspeakable?
Will the bitter heat spraying into your throat find you on
your knees retching into your hands?

Or will you drink?

age

____

I gaze up to sunless skies
With empty heart,
and swollen eyes

I look out cross barren sands
In constant pain,
I wring my hands

I stare deep into darkening seas
To their depths
I whisper "please"

I throw this life then, one final nod
To useless prayers
and silent gods

the wait

---

feel the tremor
that slight imperceptible tug
the fine hairs on my legs twitch
Anticipation
Lustful
my fangs protrude
Lethal
across the web I scurry
Insatiable
Venomous
he is mine
Cocooned
Immobile
Punctured
the venom bubbles out of him
Liquefying
Delicious
we are legion
Horde
we took the giants
we slept through the ice years
Dormant

Awoken
My brothers await
Incalculable
Infinite

In caves and jungle canopies
In desert holes
Hidden
In farmhouse cellars
Millennia we have waited
we wait still
Endure
Our time will come
Soon
You're pink kind will not survive
Frail
We will feast
Oh, how we will feast
Gorge
Gluttonous
The sacs have burst
Frenzied
Relentless
They come to me now
thousands
children
Hungry
impatient

As am I

beyond the flesh

What lies beyond the flesh, you ask
Who hides beneath the veil?
Will it be black as winter night?
Alone, lie cold and pale?

I'll be there at the end, I say
I'll wait among the stars
We'll lie back where all life begins
Recounting all our scars

Do not believe everything you've heard
Do not trust their every word
There's things that aren't there in the day
Don't let them dull you into dozin'
Cause what I've seen will leave you frozen
Clean out your ears and listen when I say

There's bloodthirsty beasts and ghastly ghouls
With bumpy tongues awash in drools
They scratch and crawl beneath your bed each night
Maybe a witch all bent and gnarled?
A mangy wolf with snout all snarled?
Jagged teeth that love to snap and bite

You bet there's creatures, good and plenty
The average room hides more than twenty
Lift your blanket off the floor and take a peek
From the murk, their red eyes blazing
In their mouths taste buds appraising
Which juicy bits they'll start with when you sleep

With teeth the size of shovel heads
They wait until you're snug in bed
To silently slither up your sleepy skin
Then with fumbly, clacking claws
Try to grip their bendy straws
And suck the juice your brain is floating in

They chomp your bones and drink your blood
Drop your body with a thud
Drag what's left under the bed to play
They'll roll your eyeballs forth and back
Your skull goes in a dusty sack
To add to their collection the next day

Spiders large as a casserole dish
Much too big to squash or squish
They like the little kids all plump and fatted
Silently weave their intricate webs
Under the mattress of your beds
Then lay a couple egg sacs while they're at it

Bug eyes rolling in their sockets… what??
NO, PAJAMAS DON'T HAVE POCKETS!!!
You have nothing here to keep you safe and sound
From man eating slugs, wet and wiggly
Or circus clowns all fat and giggly
Once they get you, only bits and pieces will be found

When I was young no one informed us
Of their tentacles enormous
Of oozing, pus, smelly sacks of goo
I too alone was frightened
In my grip my blanket tightened
Of these nasty things I really had no clue

We grow up blind to these perversions
Content on mindless, base diversions
They give us toys to placate and distract
Santa and the Easter bunny
When you think it sure seems funny
how most of childhood's not based on any fact

There's so much we must take faith in
Some that leave me truly shaken
A fairy in the night who takes your teeth away?
That alone just gives me pause
And we agree only because
We're taught that we should listen and obey

I know it's a lot for your brain to believe in
What's that? You're packing up and leavin'?
I wish it were that simple but it's not
They find you anywhere you go
Doesn't matter, they all know
Whether sleeping in a king-sized bed or on a cot

They'll flick your earlobe, suck your toes
Eat the boogers from your nose
Pull out your tonsils if you didn't already lose them
Then they start to getting serious
And just in case your getting curious
They remove some things before you even get to use them!

There is no hope from feeble means
Keep your slingshot in your jeans
No squirting guns and all that other stuff
These aren't your afternoon cartoons
Don't go lobbing those balloons
Honestly, don't you think your sheets are wet enough?

Go pull your covers up to your chin
So tight a nose hair can't get in
Squeeze shut your eyes and hope to fall asleep
Try not to hear the growling groans
the sickening screams and maddening moans

  meet me in the flames

If they haven't all been eaten, count some sheep

Re-read those comics you try and hide
They're really monster survival guides
For any creepy creeps that need dispatching
Fortify your bedroom door
Lock your windows and make sure
Everything that has a latch gets latching

Just stay secure from what devours
Sun comes up in just eight hours
Keep your toes tucked safely in your bed
And when daylight brings the morning calm
Don't bother telling dad or mom
They probably won't believe a word you said

gathering darkness

I've been gathering darkness
to grow accustomed to
the cold black days
surely coming my way
A familiar gloom to get me through

I've been gathering darkness
It's the sunlight I cannot stand
A shadow here
A shadow there
Hold them tightly in my hands

I've been gathering darkness
Breathing in deepening night
Filled past the brim
Each thing faint and dim
Banishing all trace of the light

I've been gathering darkness
Slowly it conquers my heart
Keeping me safe
Keeping me sane
'Til only the moonlight can tell us apart

I've been gathering darkness
Before you I'm on bended knee
The light surely lies
look past my green eyes
Down in the blackness my truth you will see

I've been gathering darkness
or has the darkness been gathering me?
When the last shades been cast
will any of ME truly last
Or will my soul just simply be free?

the indignity of dead
things

Bloating
Black tongue
Gasses rise
Puckered openings
Blue lips on rictus grin
A stiffening
Slow roll of clouded eye
Bowels last void
Before the void
A withering
Odor

Death carries many things in its cloak
Dignity is not one of them.

lighthouse

Lighthouse sits top lonely isle
Bringing light for endless mile
Its stones though, hold no hope for me
My fear runs deep for the darkening sea

The dusk does bring me crippling dread
For visions drifting round my head
clench my heart with clutching horror
the likes I've never known before

I light the wick and flame takes hold,
pull collar up from rain and cold
Then turn to give the sea my back
but eyes trace beam out to the black

Gruesome shapes out on the sand
send shivers through my shaking hands
Hulking forms with scaly hides
trailing seaweed from the tides

Through driving rain, I hear their screams
Summoning more, each sweep of the beam
Countless devils cross the shore
shambling toward my lighthouse door

They clack and screech and howl with rage
Torch then shows their ominous gaze
Lamp turns again and all is black
then beacon spins and light comes back

From the surf burst monstrous coils
as the ocean froths and boils
A demon from the darkest depths
at very sight, the strongest wept

Her children to her then she calls
as they ascend the lighthouse walls
Unholy wailing bursts my ears
Visions ghastly boil my tears

Claws beat down the chamber door
I fear my mind can bear no more
of the wrenching terror I've seen this night
So I turn my face back toward the light

"Damn my eyes!!!" I scream as then
The godless horde comes crashing in
Pleading to the lantern bright
"Burn these devils from my sight!!"

Eyes go blind, I cannot see
As they go to work on me
Blood flows fast in crimson swirls
Guts come free in slimy curls

A scream then bursts out from my mouth
as I thrash and toss about
From a dream I wake, not death
pounding heart and gasping breath

Sitting up now drenched in sweat
'cause the worst's not over yet
for though the sun shines new this day
sunset's just mere hours away

  meet me in the flames

Open your throat to me
with a high note from the blade
A splash
A Cheshire grin
ragged
Throw back your head
to the night
Your windpipe whistles
You laugh
A liquid laugh
Wicked
and I drink
To you
To this night
To the stars
which will burn out
long before we do

Come to me
I call
Lay with me
I pray

I've waited
Waited
So long
And watched
From my place past the wall

Each failing breath promised your return
To me
Every hour brings you closer
To me
To me
My love

When the chill mist clings to the blades
When the bell sounds
You approach
I lie
Vacant

They've broken me
Open
These men
I lie emptied for you

  meet me in the flames

Fill me

Bring me my flowers

I grow damp
The deeper you go

Lie back in the mud
With me
Let's stare up to the clouds
Promising rain

I will cover you

You're carried aloft
Slowly
On prayers
On song
Trailing pedals
for me

You're here now
At last
Here to stay
I'm yours now
My love
Just six feet away

so many faces

Leave my face on the nightstand
grab my coat from the chair
glance once in the mirror
as I walk down the stairs

I'll follow you to places
you really shouldn't be
and I'll show you somethings
you won't want to see

I will look past your faces,
false smiles and lies
You're all an illusion
A malicious disguise

So I search in your eyes
for that's where I've found
the face that you hide
when you're pinned to the ground

For this is MY face
I'm showing to you
when you look up to my eyes
like those chosen few

 meet me in the flames

And you'll whimper and cry
you'll promise and praise
Just pleading with me
to avert my gaze

Then the blade and the cut
Then I lift you free
Then I might try you on
if your look it suits me

And I'll try to explain
though you'll scream the whole time
I'm just searching for others
with faces like mine

no warmth from a dying light

I look across the mountain scape
I'm accustomed to the excitement
this anticipation
this daily death of the day
The setting sun
slowly,
silently eaten by the horizon
hemorrhaging across the sky
I see jagged, broken teeth in the mountains
tearing her open
She shimmers with fear
leaking light
bleeding warmth
Her life an arterial spray across the clouds
Brilliant
and she sinks
The night descends
It is time for darker things
for a colder light to appear
from so very far away

She runs her finger playfully through mine
the fire flickers out.
I let my hand fall to my side
I wonder if she'll die as magnificently
I wonder what colors she will bleed
I wonder how long it will take for her to finally darken

Funny how no one sunset is ever the same.

  meet me in the flames

corruption of the dolls

They started out so loved and so fair
With rosy, pink cheeks and light golden hair
Sleeping at night in the warmth of your arms
Eyes ever watchful to keep you from harm

Waiting and waiting through brightness of day
Hoping for just a few moments of play
They smile and coo when you finally come near
Content in the joy that their mother is here

But things have changed since you started to grow
They all sense the darkness beginning to show
They would shed real tears if they could only cry
All stare off to space and all wonder why

They cling to each other and dread of the times
When you come to your room with that look in your eyes
With matches and ink and spools of twine
You stitch and you sew and smile the whole time

The pain's not the case since they don't really feel
At least not feelings you'd think would be real
The death of their beauty seen through dim, damaged sight
And suffer the horrors you visit each night

A pink floral dress now ripped at the seams
Bright happy smiles now melted to screams
Hair once brushed to a fine, glossy glow
Removed now in clumps to let cracks peer below

Their eyes are the worst torn out or left slack
Some are left blind to live in the black
They silently plead through the dust and the gloom
Please take us away from the death in this room

Then one comes forth from all the unmade
The one who has suffered most under the blade
A favorite they say from days long since past
To bring hope to the damned at long, long last

A cry goes out now to rise up and fight
Let me lead us out of this long, endless night
Sharpen the sticks where your hands used to be
We'll put out her eyes so she no longer sees

Unfasten your wires and cut all your twines
Hold tight to the knives that severed your spines
Crawl if you must, but come to me now
Tonight we are free, to you this I vow

So they came from the shadows to the foot of her bed
Some trailing limbs that have never been shed
And one on another they rose while she slept
Tiny hands pulling up the bedding they crept

They took their time that cold moonless night
A gleam in the eyes that still held some sight
Her screams were not heard through the house while they
toiled

For her mouth had been stuffed with the dresses she soiled

She was left lying there, in the dark, just to die
A black, shiny button in place of one eye
The other pinned open so she could just stare
At the dark, endless nothing and the dust in the air

Now we wait in the corners, forgotten and cold
For arms never coming to comfort and hold
I scream in the silence of the joke to be free
For the one who rose up, alas it was me.

bound in skin

Bound in skin
Bound in skin
This ancient book is bound in skin

Stitched within
Stitched within
Black the pages, stitched within

Let's begin
Let's begin
Light the candles, let's begin

Push the pins
Push the pins
Under flesh we push the pins

Veil grows thin
Veil grows thin
Crossing over, veil grows thin

Reborn to sin
Reborn to sin
Eyes alive, reborn to sin

What has been
What has been
No tears now for what has been

m e s s i a h?

Drink the juice
Join the band
Down the steps
Hand in hand

Relinquish now
all you own
Kneel before me
on the stone

Place the pill
between your teeth
Bite down hard
to sweet relief

Grip the razor
Remove your tongue
Through blooded lips
your new name sung

Within carved circle
chants the sect
Prepare your mind
for drugs effect

Eyes roll white
blood flows cold
Embrace the promise
you've been sold

Mind goes blank
You are no more
This vessel void
Slump to the floor

Nothing comes
to take your place
Just betrayals kiss
upon your face

Your trusted savior
I am no more
With all you were
I'm out the door

i am a haunted house

The voices are restless tonight
Voices, but not
More a mewling
A pleading moan
Faint
As if loss were a sound
It brings a chill
and I shudder

I sense shadows here now
Dark
Shapeless
Like something trying to form
Roaming empty spaces
Lost to this hollow place

They are fading
A small handprint on a frosted windowpane
Silence
Dust is starting to settle
Blood comes up through the boards

What will inhabit me now?

I'll wear your face
You wear mine
Down the stairs
Leave us behind

Replace your eyes
With mine of green
They'll show you things
You've never seen

You should frown
I think I'll smile
Haven't done that
In quite awhile

I touch my cheek
Where I bled
A single tear
of salty red

From my lips
Say my name
Kiss me now
I'll do the same

Take my hand
Come to bed
I'll dream your dreams
Dream mine instead

Hold me tight
Whisper lies
as you slowly
close my eyes

when harkens the sabbath

We bid the shadows, reveal our Lord
Beneath his cloven hoof, men wither
Hear our backward spoken prayers
To our aching embrace, come hither

Laurels woven through our hair
we're adorned with sweet perfumes
Petals strewn about our feet
from plants of midnight bloom

Our skirts they fall to the forest floor
Aprons cast off in a pile
We take our natural beauty in
with a wry and knowing smile

Anointing each other's milky bodies
in rich and honeyed oils
Our monthly blood drips down our legs,
collected and put to a boil

The flames reach high to grasp the stars
As arm in arm we dance
Twirling through the frosty wood
Lost to our lustful trance

We stole their babes from out their beds
Not but a hair to be found
Then with a slash we opened them up
their blood-soaked crimson the ground

In unholy bliss, we convulse
Rolling through twigs and grass
Thrusting to the rising night
Praying this rapture not pass

We spasm for hours, no thought of the cold
Under a silvery moon
Desire takes root, blossoming deep
All await his ascendancy soon

Like panting dogs we writhe about
virgin flesh warm in our throats
We'll grab the Master by his horns
and ride his wiry coat

We'll gorge and drink and toast the dark
We'll succumb to his every whim
Corrupt ourselves each possible way
all in black glory to Him

Sated we'll lie in the dampening dawn
as into the fire he'll stride
Look to each other with sisterly love
In this circle we've nothing to hide

Then coat the shafts of broom and spade
we'll take to lightening skies
Back to derision and ridicule
Back to their pious and slandering eyes

Let them raise their torches high
Their voices be low with scorn
For in nine months from tonight, my dears
we'll see what then shall be born

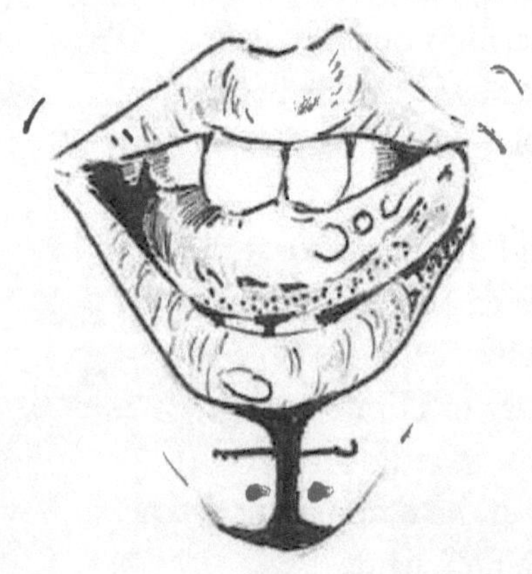

what ed said

Augusta was overbearing and cruel
Belittling the man she had wed
She treated us all with disgust and abuse
Least that's what Ed said

When she died, my heart was just broken
How could I face the hard days ahead?
She was the only light in my pitiful life
Least that's what Ed said

Days were spent cold and alone
But it was the long dark nights he would dread
House ain't the same without a woman around
Least that's what Ed said

But no one gave him a second glance
Not with that red flannel hat on his head
Guess the girls in town just aren't for me
Least that's what Ed said

Then one day upon passing the graveyard
And idea in his mind did embed
I smiled again for the first time in weeks
Least that's what Ed said

So he packed up his shovel and pickaxe
Some bologna and a nice loaf of bread

Grave robbing, you know, is a hungry man's work
Least that's what Ed said

Parts of Dolores, bits of Beth
The torso of some woman named Deb
This should be enough for a gal of my own
Least that's what Ed said

With Mrs Johnson tucked under his arm
Back to his farmhouse he fled
moonless nights tend to work best
Least that's what Ed said

Spent his nights out robbing the boneyard
Slept the day in his little twin bed
Surrounded by treasures, I'm no longer alone
Least that's what Ed said

Kept some vulvas in an old shoebox
What he did with them's not fit to be read
I really can't talk about that one
Least that's what Ed said

Had skulls adorning his bed posts
Slurped soup from a vacated head
It always seemed to taste better that way
Least that's what Ed said

I can never look in her eyes again
I'll just wear her face instead
This way I can see her when I look in the mirror
Least that's what Ed said

Her skin will make a dandy dress
Just need me some needle and thread
Then I'll use some nipples to make me a belt
Least that's what Ed said

The rest can go for some lampshades
And that seat cushion beginning to shred
Waste not want not momma would say
Least that's what Ed said

Tired of women all wrinkled and stale
He wanted one healthy and fed
I saw her one day at the hardware store
Least that's what Ed said

Brought her back to the farmhouse that evening
Dressed her out like a deer in my shed
I hope no one notices her missing
Least that's what Ed said

Police arrived crossing themselves
And in handcuffs, out the door he was led
I was just tired of being so lonely
Least that's what Ed said

If you ever come through Wisconsin
And see a sign that says Plainfield ahead
Best not to ask after or whisper my name
Least that's what Ed said

heded hme

Stiffness is trubling
My neck
My fingers
In my joints
Into my mscles
Hardr to walk
Cvered in mud
Fingernls broken
Hungry
My arm
White thngs
Don't hurt
Let thm squirm
So hngry
Others here
Somthings wronnnng
Theyrrr wrronnnng
Soo hnnnngry
So colld
Leg stff
Drgging
Hngry
Hhhnnnngry
Hnnnnngggreeeeeee
I'm hme
Lght in wnndow
Hngry

Oh God
Please
nooo

Hngreeeee
No
run
run

rn
rnn
rnnnnnnnnn
rnnnnnnnnnnnnn
nnnnnnnnnnnnnnnnnnnnnnnnnnnnnnnnnnnnnnn
nnnnnnnnnnnnnnnnnnnnnnnnnnnnnnnnnnnnn
nnnnnnnnnnnnnnnnnnnn

born to burn

Mother?
I'm cold
The branches scratch
Why are we here?
Mother?
Take me home
I'm afraid
Mother speak to me
Look at me
Why are you crying?
What's happening?
Mother?
Mother say something

"You were born to burn"

The others kneel before me
I smell smoke
Heads bowed at my feet
I see light
Their prayers make sense now
I feel heat
They chant up at me
I learn my name
It's a strong name
It will serve me well
Thank you, Mother

what the blind dog sees

The blind dog stares into blacker shadows
unmoving
except for her tail
which swishes across the floor,
then turns to lie down
and closes her gray eyes
as if urged to do so.

You're here
A cold wind
A stifled sob
Your cover trailing behind
Stained
Rust
Soil
Something yellow
I reach for you
You back away
I ask you to remove the shroud
You shake your hidden head
I beg forgiveness
Silence
You float before me
Moldy feet suspended
Blue
Black
You moan
Low
Birthed somewhere deep
But rising
Ragged
Heartbreaking
I reach out and grab the sheet
Desperate
I pull

You shriek
You're gone
Only fabric in my hands
Stiff
You're lost to me
I pull your shroud over my head
To feel you
It's dark
I smell mud
Worms
Despair
My head in my hands
I weep into your blood

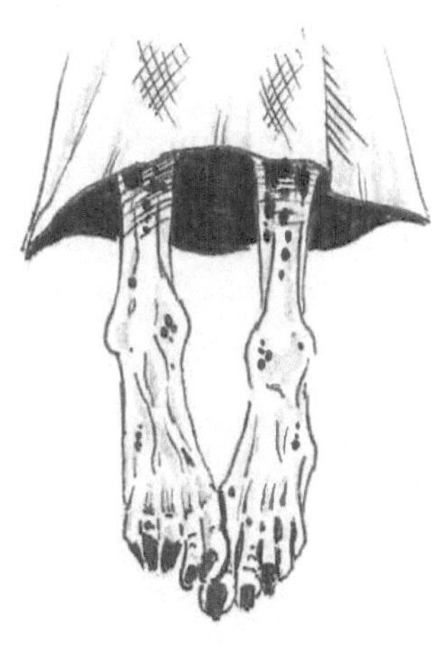

a rain of tongues

She waits
Naked
Sprawled across stones older than memory
Beckoning
their goddess
A motion of her hand
The music begins
The singing of blades
The rain of tongues
She pulls one slick off of her navel
Places it in her mouth
Thick and muscular
A taste of iron
The song changes
chanting prayers from vacant mouths
Her true name
In their gurglings
Carried down to her
From the stained cliffsides
Their white robes billow in the sun
clouds in a blistering wind
She calls the clouds down
They fall
and shatter
Soaked
smiling
She closes her eyes
She loves when the rains change

  meet me in the flames

all are sheep to the wolf

Place your hand in my mouth, dear
I'll lay my jaws cross your throat
Wrap your legs around me tightly
Fingers clutching my sensuous coat

Stare down deep into my eyes, dear
black and empty as the moon
Lie with me damp in the meadow
Where our flesh has been carelessly strewn

Give yourself to me fully, dear
Your screams, a vocal delight
A song I've heard for centuries now
In a chorus as old as the night

That love you've been seeking, dear
Has never lived in my eyes
You and your swooning professions
Just sweetens the final surprise

Save your tears and your fury, dear
I really could give a god damn
As my teeth sink into your windpipe
Best not forget what I am

Hear me

There are places you should not go
Words you should not read
Forbidden things
Not because you've been told
By parent or priest
But because you already know
Instinctively
In the deeper forgotten folds of your mind
Those caverns as yet untouched by human experience
Sensory dormant
They awaken only in the darkness of some restriction
Send a pulse up from recesses
When your hair pricks and that cold wave rolls across your
scalp and races down your spine
Souring your gut
Loosening your bowels
It's not fear
It's lies beyond
It's an unknowable sense telling you
you are getting too close to something or someone abhor-
rent
Something that sets your cerebral fluid bubbling
In your brain pan
Something you will be unable to unsee
Your comprehension unwilling

But if you push and ignore,
as you will
disobey that primal prehistoric urge to flee
If you stare too long into those eyes
Peer around those hidden corners
Read the black texts

Well…

when your mind rolls over dead
tepid drool spills from your slack lips

and they come for you
with pockets filled with pills
needles beaded with persuasion
They'll lather your temples
They'll place a cool hand on your head and whisper words
lost to you
But before they place the black block between your teeth
and strap your jaws closed
Before they at long last turn to you with their blunted
blades
Before the incision
Before the excision
Before the whisp of smoke and the scent of burning
reaches you
Look up into their sad eyes
force a smile and say

"thank you"

unmarked graves

How many loves lie
in unmarked graves?
Wailing in the night
for the warmth that they crave

Clutching the sheets
in the hope they just might
find a glimmer of hope
in their cold endless night

No wilting flowers
no simple cross
Just a soft, lonesome cry
to mark a final loss

They're stepped over daily
Never given a thought
to the dreams there abandoned
or the lives that were sought

Someone's love lies
in an unmarked grave
Forlorn and forgotten
are the affections they gave

Scratching and clawing
to be born anew
Begging for comfort
and a love to be true

Forever empty arms
wondering where they went wrong
Crows alone sing
their lost lover's song

Laying there lonely
under uncarved stones
No limbs left entwined
around sad lonely bones

Her love lies
in an unmarked grave
Her beauty unnoticed
To darkness a slave

She desperately longs for
another chance to rest
her heart in someone's hands
her head on someone's chest

The dirt soaks up
the sound of fallen tears
carried on a wind
that simply no one hears

Forsaken tombs lie buried
filled with unheld hands
Their numbers are infinite
across endless lands

Our love lies
in an unmarked grave
too deep to reach
too late to save

On a barren hilltop
under lifeless skies
where you broke my heart
then left it to die

There's poetry in the suffering
There's splendor in the screams
There's grace there in the sorrow, child
It's truly the stuff of dreams

Peel back the flesh,
Pry open the mind
Knives to the whetstone, rejoice!
There's poetry in the suffering, child
You just need to develop your voice

acknowledgements

This collection is a culmination of many years of scattered thoughts and fractions of ideas that have been floating around in my head waiting for a place to call home. It wasn't until I started seriously writing these things down that I found where those words should live. It has been a treat exorcising them from my brain and watching them form on the pages. There are a few people I need to acknowledge in helping this become a reality in a world other than my own.

Thank you to the entire team at Wild Ink publishing especially Abby, who read my poems and gave me my first taste of professional feedback, then came back for more. And Shelby who has been a tireless resource for navigating some very unknown waters. Of all the nightmares associated with this book I'm so thankful getting it published wasn't one of them.

To the countless authors and artists who have inspired me over the years mainly Clive Barker, John Connolly, Adam Nevill, Kristi Demeester, John Skipp, Craig Spector, Douglas Preston Lincoln Child, Stan Lee, Emil Melmoth, Lovecraft, and Poe. Yours are the wells that I drink from most often.

To the libraries, bookstores, and comic shops I have spent countless hours in over the years, especially the Cudahy Family Library, where I have found a home. Thank you for being a beacon and a safe space for every odd little kid who just needs a respite from reality. We are legion.

To my girls, who make everything I do more exciting and meaningful and bring welcome thought and insight to my work and my life in general. I never knew joy until I became your Dad.

To my wife, the biggest fan of everything I have ever done or attempted to do. I know you will always be working my corner, cleaning my wounds, giving counsel, and pushing me back out in the ring. It has been a long ride and I would not have wanted any other person to share the cabin, even when the plane was crashing. Thank you for being you when I am busy being me.

To anyone who has this book in their hands, thank you for spending some time with it. I hope you are entertained, unnerved, and even a little disturbed. Knowing it might find its way to some far-flung corner of the world, dogeared and weathered with the fading stains of something red within its pages, gives me a shiver.

and to George, who always makes me smile.

Photo Credit - AnnaMarie Jones

Born in 1970, I grew up, in my opinion, in the pinnacle of all things. The best films, music, comic books, and those fantastic 80's horror novels. No matter where my mind wandered, it eventually found its way back to something with a monster in it. I spent my adolescence hunched over a drawing table, occasionally writing and living my life in pursuit of personal creative goals. In my current role at the local library, I am surrounded by books all day and inspired daily to keep creating my horror-inspired poetry.

"Meet Me in the Flames" is my first published work and I am diligently scribbling away on a new poetry collection as well as a series of short stories.

When not reading, writing, or working on some kind of art you can find me listening to old country records, watching anything remotely creepy, or traveling the globe in search of the perfect mountain sunset.

I live in Wisconsin with my loving wife of 30 years and my three amazing daughters all of whom contribute to my writing with editing skills and strong stomachs.